DREAMWORKS

Trolls
WORLD TOUR

we make books come alive®
pi **Phoenix International Publications, Inc.**
Chicago • London • New York • Hamburg • Mexico City • Sydney

From his DJ booth in the underwater Techno Reef, King Trollex drops a top beat. Music brings his subjects together, so they can celebrate family, love, and, well, MUSIC! But while the Techno Trolls swish their tail fins to the rhythm, a danger lurks nearby...one that could change their techno-loving lives forever.

As all their hearts thump to the same beat, look around *one more time* for these Techno Trolls:

Queen Poppy tries hard to be a good leader. She knows that Trolls are all about having fun, but some things are serious. So when Poppy learns there are more Trolls in Trolls Kingdom, she sets off in a big flower-face balloon named Sheila B. to unite them all. But first, it's time to sing and dance and hug!

Shake your hair around Trolls Village and high-five these colorful Pop Trolls:

Satin & Chenille

Smidge

Biggie & Mr. Dinkles

Branch

Legsly

Guy Diamond & Tiny Diamond

Poppy

Cooper

Once upon a time, there was no music. Then the elder Trolls used six strands of their hair to make a powerful instrument, and they filled the world with music. Soon, the Trolls started to dislike each other's music, and the strings were divided among six tribes: the Pop Trolls, the Techno Trolls, the Classical Trolls, the Country Western Trolls, the Funk Trolls, and the Rocker Trolls.

Travel the six musical realms and find the Rocker Trolls inside the Angler Bus:

Carol

Queen Barb

King Thrash

Poppy, Branch, and stowed-away Biggie and Mr. Dinkles arrive in Symphonyville *after* Barb. The Rocker Trolls destroyed the proud, sophisticated land, stole its string, and took all its inhabitants back to Volcano Rock City—all except lonely Pennywhistle. She wants to rebuild her village. Seeing the destruction makes Biggie feel scared, but Poppy pinky-promises him that she will keep them all safe.

Help Pennywhistle put these pieces of Symphonyville back together:

cracked clarinet · smashed cymbal · Trollzart's broken baton · sprung-string violin · mangled music stand · fractured flute · crumpled sheet music · bashed bassoon

When Poppy, Branch, Biggie, and Mr. Dinkles arrive in Lonesome Flats, the Pop Trolls get their first taste of country western music. The Country Western Trolls shed tears as they enjoy a sad song. Branch points out that sometimes life is sad. But Poppy doesn't hear what Branch is saying. She thinks music should make everyone happy. And she *really really* wants to cheer up these Trolls.

Look around town for these sorrowful Country Western Trolls who **don't** need cheering up:

this Country Western Troll

this Country Western Troll

Clampers Buttonwillow

Hickory

sad Country Western Troll

Growley Pete

this Country Western Troll

Mayor Delta Dawn

Cooper sneaks a peek at the scrapbook of the history of the strings and learns there's a tribe of Trolls that look just like him! It turns out he is a Funk Troll prince with a twin brother named Prince D. In Vibe City, Poppy insists that differences don't matter. But the King and Queen of Funk teach her that denying Trolls' differences denies the truth of who they are. Heavy.

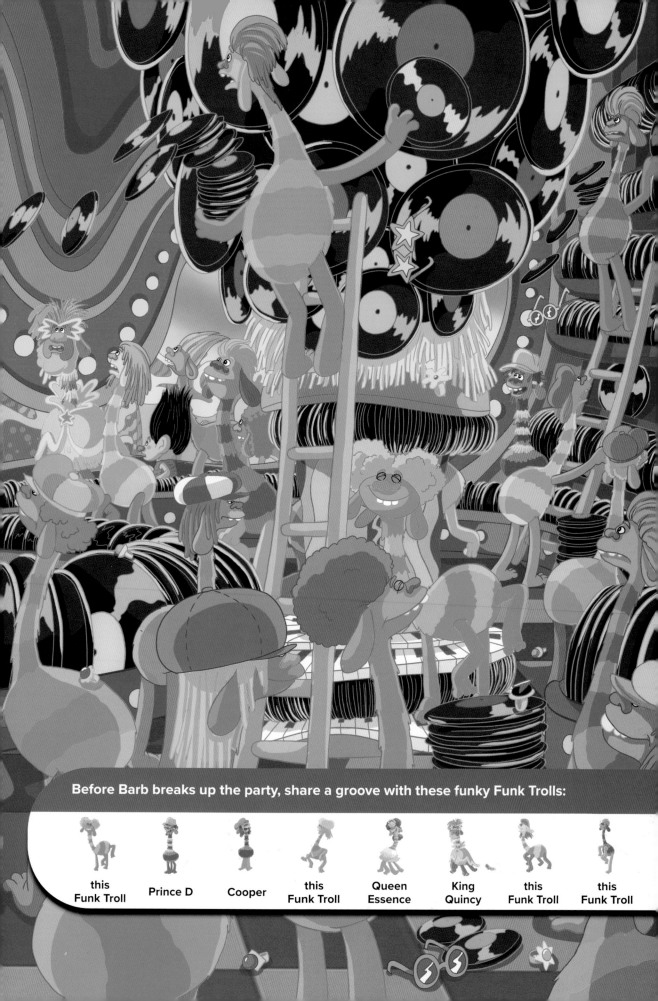

Before Barb breaks up the party, share a groove with these funky Funk Trolls:

this
Funk Troll

Prince D

Cooper

this
Funk Troll

Queen
Essence

King
Quincy

this
Funk Troll

this
Funk Troll

In Volcano Rock City, Barb plays to a crowd of Rocker Trolls as well as the Troll-napped leaders and subjects of the other musical realms. Now that she has obtained all six strings, Barb is ready to play the ultimate power chord and turn all Trolls into Rocker Trolls. Poppy has learned that harmony needs lots of different voices. Will she be able to convince Barb that a world where everyone looks and sounds the same wouldn't ROCK at all?

Put on your denim jacket and check out these Pop-turned-Rocker Trolls:

Smidge   Biggie & Mr. Dinkles   Satin & Chenille   Legsly   Guy Diamond   Tiny Diamond

Swim back to the Techno Reef and shake your tail fin with this aquatic wildlife:

Hair comes the beat! Pop over to Trolls Village and spot these Pop Trolls with pop-tastic hair:

Put on your crafting pants, make your way back to the scrapbook, and add a little extra glue to these bedazzlements:

Shred back to Barb's Angler Bus and find these wicked instruments:

ADMIT ONE

ADMIT ONE

ADMIT ONE

ADMIT ONE

Waltz back to the remains of Symphonyville and find these opening violin notes to Beethoven's 6th Symphony:

Line-dance back to Lonesome Flats and try on these ten-gallon hats:

Boogie back to Vibe City and find these funky toe rings that King Quincy and Queen Essence have unknowingly danced off their feet:

Mosh back to Volcano Rock City and rock-lock hands with 10 Rocker Trolls making the rock hand.

As Barb traveled across Trolls Kingdom, she dropped a few guitar picks. Go back and find one of her skull-covered string-strummers in each scene.